A World

Also by Dennis Phillips

The Hero Is Nothing

A World

Dennis Phillips

Cover: *Transport*, by Robin Palanker
Book Design: Robin Palanker and Laurel Burden
Some of these poems have appeared previously in *Acts*,
Archives from New Poetry Newsletter, *Main*, *Spazio
Humano* (Italy), and *Temblor*

Library of Congress Cataloging in Publication Data

Phillips, Dennis
     A World

1. Title

ISBN: 1-55713-072-8

5 4 3 2 1

This book was made possible, in part, through a matching
grant from the Cultural Affairs Department, City of Los
Angeles and through contributions to The Contemporary Arts
Educational Project, Inc., a non-profit corporation.

New American Poetry Series: 

Sun & Moon Press
6148 Wilshire Boulevard
Los Angeles, California 90048

I
On Dry Entry

A story would fill this time. Easier. To open accounts.
Fill coffers.

In this light reds and greens are the same.

Bona Fide or Fraudulent?
A clock cools. No one will speak.
Negotiations cease.

Politics and agriculture rest together,
silent, calm, empty.

□

Looked so long it vanished.

Using the word "named" instead.

A declamation devoutly to be wished.

Force of Helios powering upwards.

What will be left if I am left?

On a cloud- and lifeless boundary.
A tempest coming alive at night.
Critical match.

Each letter.

□

A section of the vital shoulder
opens secretly to the heart.

A landing, christened, held obsolete but worshipped:
Plymouth Rock, John O'Groats, Tierra Del Fuego.

An older lesson, born of vulcanism:
Lava tubes pumping from the core
new extremities.

Don't look at me: If the fire escaped
even hope would vanish.

□

Damaged clouds.
An ovum clinging to ladened weather.

No fragment preserves silence.

In acceleration, in pregnant dark, clear.
Release is blurred, edges softened.

If I watch this long enough.

An idea in the form of a story
beginning with an ending, histrionic, sad,
a tragedy, inevitable, but false, a mirror
not false, not a mirror.

□

LOSS OF PRESSURE (1)

Sudden loss of pressure.
Tendril severed.
A card floats ashore.
A casket, a stack of hay bales.

Whose job would it be? Fields
of well worn parts.

Every call hooked up.

The house full of smoke.
You say pressure, pressure.

☐

LOSS OF PRESSURE (2)

Tired. To a pin point. Nature's balm.

Or freeze the metal snaps off
in strangling blue, pure sky.

Sudden loss of pressure,
Replaced with nothing.

Falling scar. Numb.

□

From adhesive. Instead of blood.
A transfusion of venom.

> M'amour, M'amour
> What and where?

The walls adhere, glue electric.

> You cannot take from me
> anything that I will more willingly
> part withal

This rent a worse wide one sodden, incarnadine.
The spiders have gotten here first
what their mandibles sucked out their webs can't clog.

□

Doll-perfect dark face
at mother's breast

Unchanged but grown
at her own breast to suck

As if my flu were aggression
suddenly all hell, a fever, casts out.
No harbor. No soothing stream to cool.

Under a fern an icon
her eyes wood her nipples flesh
perfect dark face a harbor.

And times when only wood

□

The old woman called your fever.
You knew she was dead.

Her voice grabbed into your skin.

You kept thinking of a building
so vast it held marshlands.
Dense reeds and high then
endless corridors.
There was an office you needed
but a pulse brought you to.

"Touch me," she whispered.
"To keep the fever back."

You expected dry, hard leather
but her wrinkles were tender.
"Now tell me what you feel."

"Reeds," you said. "A pulse."

□

Laughing that the skull was bolted to his desk he'd
been trying to pry it off, the invisible
jewish skull.

A cat would cry and this would empty,
river's final phase.   Seasilt saltsick.

The gravity of the single written thing
pulling randomly: image, motive, masque.
So little literary.

☐

But a delta, finger of cocktips a new
gravity where things stand, press against
verticals.

From a window cones and rods
lying against a chess board resting
against a wall.

She comes in her room grey floorboards
a trace of rope, grecian dress.

Now listen closely it's about sex in one spot
was it you she spoke of or someone else how
good it was tied down, supine, roped
to the floor.

You respond to some wide permission
with ideas of crime.
But she's out by then, hot and searching.

You seem to be holding your erection and
humming a Phaiakian work tune
        They bore him back, so fast, so fast,
        Asleep, toward home, at last, at last

□

My hands sweated stickum but no web came out.

"It's only an idea," I said.
"No hourglass on your palm."

But a small hole, rind of blood, lipless tiny mouth.
It wants to speak but it's empty.

Or a clumsy finger at a fragile egg,
a pointy adhesive tongue.
What seemed arachnoid is avian.

"This cannot be mine," I cried.
"It can't be your hand."

Cold metal on the temples
inside, on the tongue.

□

Her decision against self-slaughter but her guess
at what she forfeits
cut from the story
fragments of concern.

Was it a field of jasmine (grave day)
or mulched oak leaf (high electron)
his foot pressed into?

Why *not* prose?

Now we can't find her.

He writes this.

□

He awoke in a crowd that stared
into a giant light or fire. No voice dismissed them.
No compacted or tilled soil detained them.

To find himself across a continent
surrounded by singles bars and convenience stores.

There had been troops but he escaped.
Down the steepest hills
from barren housing tracts
to overgrown truck farms
to where he couldn't be found
he fled.
His sister's last words "You'll be killed"
dropped behind.

Sad farewell to familiar scapes.

His gestures now his own among strangers.
A light or fire, a signal. "Notes," he says again.
"Only notes."

□

Your glistening back
up from warm water
our underview
shallow, bright, lexicon of creatures.
Esperanza waited naked in our room.

We were all so patient.
You were lovely and indulgent.
She exhibited herself but would not be touched.
I might have known this, but forgot.
We abandoned her

and will remember instead a large black manta ray
and I the touch of your hand
warm in the cooler sea.

□

Europa seduced rides isleward.
Details cover her.

She would say to you that which
took away. Each word a minus.

Warm wind shrouds her arms
estival, noon, tired, calmed
a smooth moment where rough once was.

She would hold up a condom.
Remember her eyes?

Currents sweep in. A Crete we can't find
still sends its missives.
Her arms freed, even as the divine bovine
swims out to sea

the beautiful, reillusioned warm one astride.

□

Feet your feet
flooded entries
particular entry

and in the recesses
(your domain, past)
closets well-stocked but chaotic.

Portable sex paraphernalia
secreted to a cool grotto
red walled and green.

A child is hacked apart
who then grows back from a soup.

On dry entries emptiness.

You return to your room.
Sound removed. Closet drawers
filled with pastels.

Portable grotto. The face not the face left.
The house not the house.

□

They would these lips kiss
the invalid's mouth

a scene rendered humid
oppressively humid

the order of envelopes determined
and who would face whom at table

fetching her to join the company

no limbs allowed or needed
only the fantasy of danger an
old vestige losing strength a quieter dictum
covering over.

□

In a dream you would fall from a ladder.

The space is not deep or shallow
a speech you heard in a new courtyard.

An herb you once burned
on the pinpoint of a probe
But fall?

The ladder tips.
Balance at the top.
It's you falling, new bricks rising
impact cushioned, harmless.

It was made for you to notice
that the words must hold
something you missed last time.

There were two large Noguchi stones.

You remembered hunger.

□

But you had the coffee.

(No one had)

The cuckqueans
our projections, we
bearers of weapons
entitlement, power.

No one had coffee.

————————

Your hand brought persimmons
face drank mouth spoke
eyes looked away.

What was blamed on weather?
Fatigue, lined skin, a feeling of malaise.

What office? The office of delay
the office of detour
averted eyes, single purpose.

———————

They will have you sit and wait
then drink their beverage.
They will forget then remember
fetch and bow, stand and conclude.

Their contempt or confusion or doubt
will be hidden in accessories:
desks, blinds, new phones,
highly erotic amanuenses.

———————

Highlighted edge.
       *He showed a white cheek
       over his shoulder.*

Your bright chest
against my flannel.
No masque.

□

The nephew awakened

parts won't fit
one over one under.

Face peers in.

Summer
day dark storm
impatient sea.

A room where others wait
awake but deadened.

□

Dark storm day but hot
dark noon grey, sea grey.

Any calm disrupted ions
charged or pressure dropping
too quickly inside cool floors
grime of sand summer house.

Sleep, sister of drugged stupor,
hooks tiny hesions
but in the blood sea
through windows now
darker, the weight
inside the eyes.

□

Cold autumn
waters clear tropical blue wild
dog jumps from the boat
        snags a gull, is hauled aboard
        with quarry.

        The waters are warm. But no steam
        whorls off the surface, clear shallows
        giant sunfish hover below.

A flimsy pier hovers above.
From there the water's an inlet, close-mouthed
silver light on the boat the pier
debris against green volcanic wall.

        Passive fish, tiny wings.

2
Ilium of Protection

Saw one dashed by cruel waves
saw tanks of air saw hotels
saw walkways leading to popular museums
unrated but stringy arms (mine)
lowering him (me) down
glowing wet ink, cables,
long distance.

Saw a bedroom and women outside
saw women in duos who entered
saw a suite of rooms
saw a bedroom immune to sound
but heard the breathing in grey weather
pounding, grip, suction.

The husk to this was very cold.
We called for a propane standard;
too feeble, too feeble.

Dank a.m. Cold took sound.

And closed, slept, nil
to a place not easy but still with hope.

We held our arms out.

A secret fluid filled each one
the vulnerable succumbed to residue
and residue became obsession.

The powerful don't need conspiracy.

An abstract trill regarding law and punishment
robbed still sleep. Will darkened.
Who is this person you've kept from us, they inquired.
They knew it as your accusation.

□

Hills or ladders, tracks, rings
        doused in the breeze of the sea
        washed in salt and windward, coastal
measures against skill and endurance.

"Do you want me?" Asking negates action.

It is the trial by climbing which beckons.
O we'd been there before when houses crowded the shore, chic,
well-furnished and through their sliding kitchen doors the sea.

Gone now.

Trestled dunes.
Stark shore.

□

1

(Scherzo)

The names of grammar came in.
Their rules disguised
great violence around them.

Each hat was a day and many hats many days.

Great books spilled from the names
the door to the cabinet Onan
closed in their honor.

Any bell whatsoever threw them into a rumble.
Whose side are you on Mo-fo, asked they of thou.
"Hast heard my name aforetimes?" You
from a fantasy of an orgy of reading
answered not.

Mutations commenced:
"When two vowels go walking
the first one wears the stockings"
or
"I before E except when you pee
but never in harbors and never on me."

The hats of their clothes fell dead
but the hunt among them was cancelled.

Great violence flared, their red, orange, filings of blue
smacked, washed up, exploded, faceless merging,
hats falling, color spilling from their great books.

A bell split them then stopped them
a history measured in billions receded, heads and hats
pooled in a butter sillier and sillier.

Yellow is a primary and red
and blue. When two vowels
are E one must be dead.
Nothing in its life became it like the leaving it.
Henceforth be earls.

2

The plain of Elpenor
at the pit of Tiresias

a hat for each day
a quivering jugular of black ewe
for each hat.

Plates and plates of volcanic slab
smooth, terraced layers
down to the shore in slag
to dark hellcurrents or name the river.

Enter.

What any of the ghosts
prove by their entrance
otherwise a waste that speaks
future perfect.

Black hull departing
no mark in these waters.

3

Plates, dull wood, thin
strata to the pit

Sword hewn, black woodsoil

those who have led us here
but not been here

Nell mezzo

pity of error
pumped black blood
to voice the prophet

Find them deep sleeping
whose voices
call up, arch over
for someone
to take down

4

His book merely cold to visits

This society of monument or absence
this cold snowbound eastern.

But whose context? A trajectory
again and again

over a wooden continent.

Waiting all day to free a word chain.

To know face as typeface
a silence, a high voice.

Directions.

Fragmatics of the landmass

Mercy of traveling it stops
moving the voice stops the scenes
inside stand aside for views outside

movement, painless, movement

Slept in bushes, woke to a ball
naked servant girls,
most virginal leader,
your salt-caked shoulders

An emporium of passage
say the right thing
(part of the plan)
the plot no more complex than
people will do as they must
then find salvation (what relief).

Who took you home?
A rock remains once rowers and racers

an unrecorded oar
somewhere inland, noted, unidentified
at the foot of the temple of some god
of some thing called the sea.

□

Sat back.   Pulse pulsing.
False lead.   Too obscure.

Old ones steal young ones copy

Then: a swirl of pipes
and inaudible jabber a
romantic garden covers soft sand

Enthusiasm, late, an interminable hour (digital display)
Imagine Cuchulainn drowned on a swirl
of an Andean piper's tune.

Enthusiasm can't be separated from envy.

A garden's statue of cold false-marble
from a tundral plain, from a fog bank.

Sudden buckling, a whip of Italian,
temperature of green glass
Giardino Romantico, a beaten old pier

pulsing steady against blue pulse
the fast chop inside a reef or barrier wall
a romantic harbor, stolen.

□

And we stuck with the irresistible vestige
of using code.

Angry eyes appoint guilt. Bystanders hold ice to napes.

Your name is called from a dissolving border
a woman in a dark sari warns of her irate spouse
so handsome, she says, that he believes his own version
only.

Smoke has settled around the survivors
(everyone survived)
the husband appears, ugly and mad.

The crackling fuse, you deny.
The harmless game, you deny.
The celebration of sport, you deny.
It had all been sanctioned. It was part of a plan.

The smoking dud, you deny.
The billows of choke, you deny.
Fleeing but avoiding dangerous alleys, you deny.
It had all been sanctified. You match ire.
We hapless victims. Happens? or mystery?
An image for each element.
We will never be caught.

□

Begged for it back
nasal electric.

A crab on his face.

The announcements rolling: constant command.
We love "command." Love crabs' sharp skeletal.

The speaker at your door. His face
only a voice, nasal electric.

"I am humus. This is the season.
Bury me."

But walks on waiting,
pictures the streets empty.
Pictures acceleration
from a low angle (shot off a shovel).

Command ignored, sharp processes ignored,
we adore command, adore the shells
and steel tombs
and passing announcers.

Whose face gutted by carbon
begged for it, begged for it back.

Not in the lightless announcer's cabin
no crab there

but the comforting phantom pain the wish
"Turn out my burden.
It will serve no one else.
No questions will be asked. This is the season."

You won't speak.
Streets as he pictured.

□

All for your red eye
devil drink yr ink

looked red then green
looked black
the ink
black in its flask

Your carmine fear of it
or alone and slack-jawed death

unzipped (&) rattling, opened and pried open
devil ash and angel rock: black pumice and red eye.

Sharp edge too fast

Take the mirror away
those eyne too orb too lucent

too iridesce that single red now green
It spoke, spoke too much, inky

touch, no toucht not, single now
it spoke, spoke too much, red, green touch

for your eyne, take the mirror, cold stone.

□

This was reportage and no one kept a progress.

Who will they think a thief if not an innocent?

This was a total surprise. The milk bar seemed secure.

What voice we asked what voice transmits orders?

Picture a verdant sector somewhere east
a summer picture, but with a roof.
Bring all confessions there

which make reasons nothing.

Breezy, chaotic weather. The face appears
possessing the voice, an hermetic thief, tucked among clouds
surprised at its own, confident in its cunning.

□

Then he a bureaucrat became
a Nosferatu and pasty white.

His fears a caldron boiling his
feet bergs of ice (so, so cold).

The price of ambition, he said
the altruistic rationale, pale, translucent.

A trick of the eyne, the horizontal
or vertical? Which direct?

These curries, this cur of world.
And said yes, and also more.

□

But other things came in. A different tidy
work-force (singular). The hoarfrost and thanks
for morning. A tingle in the wrong appendage.
A stream of noise skyward indicating a population
never graspable.

Never pictured himself a bureaucrat (can't spell it)
but threads steam up a new demanded tangle
an agility to spread them evenly, re-weave them,
turn them into something, call them ambition.

And other things: Three foot-long lines of semen
on her chest, retracting distance, last
closest to him, on her for example of hormones
stream of genetic fluid a populace possible,
father of thousands, floating flower,
ribboned wife.

□

On this plain to the sea fog en-
crusted sunless morninged the small
of it a whisp in the air but inland
far enough to be distant
but near

the slope in your mind
a pebble in your thinking
gradual scoop to continental shelf.
This pebble on your land-locked street.
Inhabitant of a coastal zone

ready to ship out, spoils divided, a decade of tilting
City of the Plain from City of Tents.
Gravel in your shoulder, gravel in your bedding

Henry Five's easy Ilium
Whiles yet the cool and temperate wind of grace
o'reblows the filthy and contagious clouds
back to the city. Fresh air in your face.

□

And fog soft night harbinger summer soft
soft lips bare skin soft
season of fog precedes season of temperate nights
vernal to estival, specific
to the city of the ocean's plain

Worship at which shrine believing in none
but adoring the buildings and masks, ceremonial axes,
sharp ceremonial chairs

Came in a wave of sleepspeech
the body walking the brain heavy
in an ecstasy of sounds. Was the temple the goal
where only a wall remains
at midnight driven through the labyrinth
the ancient city in deep shadows, in sleep
to roll a tongue of paper
in a chink of stone wall

Request? demand? curse?
then rushing back through internal alleys and stepways

Plain awash, acid droplets and base
young white fog
to arrive at a bastion
unlikely yet craved
and at the fences
drink in the fog
cool and quenching

□

Found your island play
in time to be occupied elsewhere
in time for fogs that prove
new weather.

We said you were someone otherwise distracted
and held up a number of models to compare you to.
None worked which left us staggered in a desert
near a long runway we had built hoping you could fly.

You know the players
your pawns and rocky elements and barren
a place to seek vengeance
for a lifespark you claimed to taste
in this indelible fog.

□

Then wind came and time
shellshocked silence a wide stare
words as icons
fire blown out on altars.

Then from the east
an opaque weather sandy and obsessive
each layer a theme in a long repetition
where no vampire can light its buzz
too feeble in the currents.

Time shelled to powder applied to blank
but sweating faces, crushed powder
laden with residue
heavy metals, half-life thousands, pulverized
calcium just a fraction of the wind
opaque and whining,

season imposed.

□

SACRIFICE (1)

Gave your sacred element to the air and wilted
or your fluids to an ether and dried quietly away.

A voice a single line, spawned from a word
a sound a quiet; looked for a category.

Who shouted: Come down little sir
come down. The pitch is too steep
you don't have the balance.

And you stayed put the sea breeze
the view, your veins opened
passing the gift eventually to ground
in thanks
            bleeding pale tribute

But foresaw your footing and made it, sutured tight.

Water in great square reserves
returned your loss but bluer
and cooler than you had given it.

SACRIFICE (2)

Eyes through a veil
circled a voice not used
not used to this aggressive tone

eyes averted to sunlight.
Circled in frost a comment we didn't expect
not in this context
unrelenting self-promotion (what a shock).

The gauze in a calm night light
a sodden, petrified sleep
covered over in wet cloth
and shocked to see
you were once so dry, once compliant.

Bright the blue hand shadows
we expected so much else
and only fog came, grey that gauzed us
our holiday not fine, no trip to the lighthouse

□

SACRIFICE (3)

We were asleep and a specter knocked
hands of purest adrenalin and a voice

Hundreds of forms filled us
but the contents spilled

> Step, step, step, outside the stranger's footfalls
> vanished. His face at the door had been
> embarrassed, hiding behind a rounded jocular
> screen. Now he was gone, his silly conceits of
> blindness and poverty were gravel swept from
> the walkway

At a time when neighbors ignore upkeep
and sirens continue deep in the background
Hoarfrost grip thy tent, thankful night spent
and gripped in a cold edge, a metal papercut
these few things.

□

An Illiad of protection the rules suspended
by whims and lusts

You waited in a Judean tent
held your black curls overhead
desert wind a shawl you wore

Black, red, mirror, gold

While the hero sulked the sperm surrounded
pecking and whipping, pecking and whipping

We as gods adore our flung components
watch and root with a new recombinant confidence

In that light the slight bow of your neck
tiny arrows embedded in the cloth of your blouse

Your bare thighs spread open enclosed in Judea

lips (care lesse lips to misse) apart
full lips a word no only gesture
(gold to ayery thinesse beate)

You issued complaints as protection
our red eye looks in on the action
pecking and whipping till none get in too
complimentary

Your pelvis the world
where this revolved.

□

Light gentle bow today a new curve
hot light glass trapped
decrease the glands' speed

your bare thighs strong parting
letters won't cure this
nor hashing over who will answer and who will not

only the tepid warning, never precise
never understood.

He waited to drain all adrenalin
and drink it from a tumbler.
There's the lighting. Where's the god?

You explode upward in the season of ash
one of a thousand types of gum tree
in the dry ashen season
happy in the dark full moon
heat

your water caked in clay
your round leaves prospering

This is a State day
ceremony and rhetoric

You explode upward in dry thermals
grey green against night coal
explode in stasis
ever outward ever frozen
and frozen in heat
upward in ash heat
in dried heat
in your season
driest residue.

□

3
Alone Than Light

What complex thing
dark land to visit?

Black sky in daytime
fields of rubble then mountains
the air so clear there is none
the blue so deep
no water.

But rubble then stiff ranges
a Katmandu we call lunar
or a flat; sophisticated irony.

The succession is a succession of dark-haired girls
her bruises always in the same place.
A banner (slogan and music)
teases above her head beckoning her (them)
to follow.

When they speak they speak a laughing dialect
too pathetic to sit alone too potent
to be ignored. Bruised in the same spot
identical clothes identical skin only one
(surprise) only one in the darkland,
lunar, high contrast.

It was then we found air
let her clothes float slowly to the rubble.

In the next scene she was nothing
not a judgement but a stranger.
Her eyes contained a new x-ray.
We left alone.
Then light.

□

Because it hurts when you're in me.

The rhythm of wipers, of rain
made me dizzy so swoon

That's if: epilepsy or Bell's palsy
lurking inside

not to be conjugal, these fibres which
drive me out of my bed my wicked
endometrium paring me, shunning you

Rhythm of vipers combing the basket
song of the piper erecting a charm for me
then paralysis

Until the spell comes on
tiny mouth cramped ghoulish
and the foam breaks forth
from frozen lips

Spittle my diamonds.

Feel for me. I'm a boulder
a coral a buried root.

□

Her breasts must have been offered.
A coat of oil. Her desire.

And yet she stopped short.

A group of middle class adults who didn't belong
were waiting.

Legal action had been threatened.
This was part of a dispute you knew nothing about.

Outside one of the women implicated you.
Three-thousand dollars, she said.

It was your parents' apartment not yours.
You intercepted your father.

He knew about the legal action.
He was obviously in the right.

Your anger did not subside.
Three-thousand had nothing to do with it.

She refused again.
What would it take to convince her?

Several brown hawks dove from the air.
Far too late in history to pay them mind.

□

On a windy mesa.

You walked on a bare mesa.

Near a landing strip.

And waited.

You had not been there before
or not there for a long time.

In the distance a motor.
A deep note vibrating.
You held the sound to you.
To your pelvis.

Alone.

Pleasure.

□

You called your heart a flutter
not a beat recalled your
hand which touched its chest
but dug in harder or a gland
deep inside.

It wasn't violence
it was writing.

And "This" is an easy reference
contained, fragment
of a world.

Where the heart will be the whipping boy
the way a dream will speak in opposites

the way you might finger an adrenal
but it's innocent, just responding.

Water drips then sprinkles, showers down
a dark slab. Angles, double angles, triple
spring apart and light filters and wet jungle air
blankets you this morning removed but still wresting.

Might have given you a retreat
but you and your "civilization."

□

Evening. Dark over
under trees.

Four days never really fit
onto a page.

She was humid her skin
humid her lips

and the others
and the guest of honor
warm in the hidden moisture

And it felt good but you quietly scratched at a screen
splintering your nails, trying to escape
although no one would have stopped you.

But she followed you.
And her leggings.
And your fingers.

□

Eats a pudding that's waking
and wakes.

Chin presses against throat
where the parathyroid would be.
But this is August, no one around.

It was an Italian satire
in which the word micturition
was used often, often gaining laughs from the audience.

The pudding was made of ants.
Their foraging is constant, the myth that they stop at sundown
a vestige of lunar-based calendars.

Sleep takes on too great a significance
waking becomes hateful, the fear of death
becomes an aberrant contradiction.

There is an alliance
that puts you off or won't take you in.
And what you desire.

□

The voices that were left
had names
a name on each voice

Dolorous.

                    Each name
                    sent you off

and off means other names

On one chair in a void
you only cried
to bring a word
from your dead father

and only your words

Lakedaimon, wide planes
Eurykleia, hidden larder
Tiresias, permission, exit

A par

One score and schema
a name sent to
Pythagoras

More math thou transmigration.

□

On the floor where the goddess.

In the air.

Connective tissue yields a malady
or a membrane, passage.

Her eyes sunken.

Or it was water
under pressure in pipes
timbres hummed
and you said
"Harmony" and said
"So sublime" then
"Lovely" but meant something
serious.

The house alive.

As: where she slept.

And where she slept all
symptoms matched up.

Things were touching:
Vibrations earned sound

the house a tuning fork.

The goddess slept on middle C
frequency, amplitude
timbre, decay

You said "Whose small mouth
did you attach?"

But this air.

□

SURVEY SURVEILLANCE

(1)

The shelf of rock
the layers of rock, rock ridges

The keeper we have watched
the keeper in green

Coat and pants

Read this in several months to people
who might be there

The top about to blow off
but the man in green
on the shelves of rock

Because adrenalin's electric,
shelves volcanic

Who came from his hut angled against
wind and rain. Horizontal world.

A tiny oven, but electric. A crucible
and an eyecup full of molten metal.
An eggcup then, if eyecups don't.

From where each day I'd observe him
dressed in green walking
from the neat lumber of his cottage
to the rough strata that feathered off
to a wet landing at the water.

No amount of adrenalin could.
Or any amount, so.

His record evidently by lantern light
until dawn. Ash leaf after ash leaf.
History? I wondered.

And named a name.
And was seen. And was stuck in a moment.

Dressed in fatigue. Layered in stone.
Confused between a taut musical line
and a plumb line. Lyric and narrative.

Layered in stone. On stone.

One temper or tempered line.
Annealed in steam and water.
Water then steam.

First he's static.

(4)

Only thought a motor held by thread
a backlashed head a day at Inca pyramids

then slap, fresh storms
strong water on black rock.

Dressed in fatigue.

Letters to the vanishing point.

No amount of adrenalin could.

If the day would be fine then.
Cold bodies plunge into ocean.

From where each day I'd.

Or from the next landing see him.

Persistence of memory.
As if he really moved or I.

□

We live in a city.
But this one has streets.

Layers. A sheen.
A dozen million assassins.

And a rain so acid
a mile later; a thousand miles later.

We drive on the streets
a thousand dry footings this time,
summer and incredibly
no one can remember which street.

Once there was a man like a wall
so tall so wide and now
a city. We live in a city.
That's us now. Housed in a mirror.
That's us looking.

□

The calibrate who come
a wind or a set of windows

Gobi of height or grit

She opened her blouse and
we calculated a wind
in a picture
that needed solidity

This mechanism of distraction
not a start but a box

You're looking for a positive illustration of it
but that's in structure not compliance.

□

An arrest of

cloud of shawl

thin of strata.

Who holds a card under
and listens above? Who
listens above and calls out to one
to a dozen empties?

The sudden clearing and you.
You sit admiring.

A countenance that hovers
like someone's dream, midday
in a metal-fused bridge
letters due and lists

Come to the crucial. Calm down
to the crucial crossing.

You may explain to them that the coincidence of holidays
destroys their quaint beliefs and they'll be angry each time.

Or haze destroys the vista.
Day lanterns. Latent day.

One tongue not nearly enough.

□

Your whole embrace
whole embrace

One of the things I would do
cut by a swath of fog
into a form you never recognized
two heads two sets
of eyes

More an actor and I'll look on.
Your death a dozen ways only
my fear of it

A beam through

one shade one shadow
and dusty light all corona

and crown the crown she said
above her only body
this close

through air/grit but cold
time will not can not rush this
frozen, separate

a coil
through one crown and through
your likeness

Taste your close
eyes mouth hands
to lose

Your cause.

My cause.

No lip or language
too far.   and hence.

Welcomed and off welcomed.

Rest now.

□

While some too sweet melody and
too hot room full.

Dance.

This increment, "tiny toothsome morsel"
O hallmark, O reporters, and style.

Because instead they walked for hours
just for a glimpse or breath
and came to a beach, turned around
did not glance.

And stone, metal, fabric of some kind
cool steel light long column not silver
not gold.

A salon and compact crowd
each element at 98.6
creates a tropic
palms possible snow outside.

Some music.

Too late to minuet.
None of these pieces will fit back in the box
and if that seems hopeless.

☐

LOSS OF PRESSURE (3)

Some wool nappy
nurses' fingers flood of mystery

that cold hydrant, circles down
silent cyclones, aerodynamics
fluid dynamics, ocean's deep wells

rivers push a cold cold
why they weep that way

a fireball when silent weightless expected

Architecture extemporaneous
small fragments bone and flesh
pieces of cold wool

down in the frigid
where volcanic heat wells

sorry hydrant
new creatures
too deep for fire

☐

LOSS OF PRESSURE (4)

Hurtling through.

Sudden nil first heat
then sudden nil

then
how it happened
only the living

Loonely in me loneness

And all without sound.

□

To read it again to check it.

No violence would prevent them from repairs.
They must be made.

Finally the instructor loses patience
berates shocked students.

Yards and yards of water
blue and warm, again and again.

Fatigue will close our eyes
but inside voices contend.

The voices contend and then
the words are repeated.

Check it. Check it again.
These artifacts so pathetic.

One cold room. And now this.

□

A bridge on a cold Soviet river
but the warm water steams.

Nor a wild tipping rabbi
on shtetl roof but a poet
on rafters

Just western gravity
approval a latter-day phenom

Only doubt against it (gravity)

So we toss it over
house falling in a litter
of chickens and cows
all floating in arctic cold
down to the hot Volga.

□

Where no rejoinder would change their minds
mere opposition, a politic micro to macro.

A great writer in her stone cottage
a neat wood beyond, a helper spinning wool inside
the writer knew you
embraced you in emerald light.

To explain her use of history.

Or your cavalier use of narrative.

Where no description of some broader scope
would seem of interest.

The mention of a specific word a
too familiar "du" could cause violence
or on national television "fuck" or
"asshole" riots.

Amphitheater of an age: lens and electrons
a "forum" controlled inside, issuing through wires
or waves (beams?) millions of citizens.
Computerized pins and electronic grids:
sight to the blind their first paintings
sold through the air waves.

A stone cottage, a rebuttal.

Cold smell of sacred stone.
No approbation for you
except you were there.

□

Woke in Alhambra under
Moorish Idols
          under the green sea

in 600 AD a Jew
among Berbers

A glimpse
when thought and craft

when Blacks and Jews

☐

<u>My Mosque</u>

Your sandy skin

a moorish wall
beneath

or a general of Venice

The stark of rock and a
central plain devoid of orchards

and a city of arches and Mosaic
Maimonides in full aphorism

Sunny and populous

a dim memory

start with title.

□

There's a place and it's a crater
malignant beyond chemicals and radium.

There's no incision to excise it.

And it's not just one side of an argument

Because the place breeds explosions
and murder and the home of the destroyed
breeds the next destruction.

Only a boat on a sea safe
steel waters, perpetual pacific

touch land, take water, set off

Adrift, lightless on black ocean.

□

You call and the fabric collapses.

Faint expectation, please cheer me,
then plain, flat

missiles were shot again today
at first toward rumors then
the body of their leader was found.

Some deadly genetic construct is released
message from dying organ
to kill as much and more
win a bright spot

then silence, call dispatched
to plain tone, howls
dismissed, too weak, too strong.

It may be true that it's all about
amassing an audience that thinking beyond that
is only a decoy

or it may be that some fluid
chokes us off so sharply
only a decoy would save us.

They hold up dead daughters
then everyone hangs out their dead.

Nothing is solved.
Only the arena enlarges.